MW01171015

Angel King

Jami Lynne

Copyright © 2023 by Jami Lynne

Library of Congress Control Number: 2023905636

ISBN 979-8-9895869-0-5 (Ebook)

ISBN 979-8-9895869-1-2 (Paperback)

ISBN 979-8-218-15846-0 (Hardback)

ISBN 979-8-9895869-2-9 (Audiobook)

Published by Whiners Press

First edition November 2023

Book design by Dijartsy

Editing by Vanessa Dremé

www.jamilhiner.com

to eternity...

2019

He came to me while I slept. Each weighted step brought forth the impending wreckage as the ground crumbled in his wake. He proclaims only half of him bleeds. I wish to taste the drippage of these cuts brought to me through blood-stained cloth. For it is I, he wished would carve his skin with intricate patterns in the likeness of those embroidered huipils from indigenous tribes. Skin sliced and sewn back together like a lattice on his favorite pie. Our mark upon this place is like none before, and not to be replicated.

It's cold out, Demigod. The frigid air rips across my cheek like the talons of a vibrant dragon shining with prismatic splendor.

His scent burns through me like a freezing brand on a winter day. His breath, as cold as ice, yet hot as the summer sun, perplexing his goddess. She is not free; he is not free in the typical sense. However, vastly freer than she.

It was scorching hot the day I arrived. I saw the ashes. They fell as I walked feverishly across the broken desert terrain. Bare feet but unharmed by the smoldering heat.

We are unaffected by the geographical isolation of Earth. We cannot be isolated. We cannot be divided.

A mesmerized entanglement of our labyrinth. I stood behind him, looking forth. We peered ahead at the wall of stone. We couldn't reach its height nor could we extend our arms to its length. An intricately woven maze of stone. We inferred that there was no signage, no exit, and no light. It is we who must decipher the route. The others looked to us for guidance. He exclaimed, 'he leads' I let him lead but I do so aside him. Never in front of or behind my Demigod, always aside.

Fireflies light the ground like flickering bulbs of disorderly tediousness. Luminous twinkles speak stories through the night sky, a lullaby of sorts we hear. The stars are dying, the planet's dead, and the comets are teasing us within our heads. Rhetoric so destructive yet peaceful still, it's calming the places within with shrill. I stop to contemplate our earthly connection. Why does Earth's matter cause such torment? What difficulties lie ahead? Can a goddess occupy a fraction of space within your realm?

Tick, Tick, Tick the stopwatch hands move rapidly. *Click*, she stops the watch to savor this space in time. She does not know how long it will last and she doesn't ever want it to end.

I'm not made of rainbows, butterflies, and blue skies. I'm of volcanic glass spewing obsidian into the sky, on a one-way spiral down a fiery highway. As I cool, I spread over him like a warm blanket. Tucking him in for a long slumber, one I never wish to wake from, if that is what I must go back to.

I shudder at the thought. I place his hand in mine, skin is soft. I wince when I reach to touch the wing, fire ablaze the tips. I think of those that stood in my place before me. Their insignificance, humiliating and ripping through the wind. Were they mirrors of insubstantial locusts unfit to reign? Or were they mere mortals trying to catch a glimpse of a god at work?

Thick skin necessary for survival. The scales are vibrant optics with variations of silver, rose gold, and royal blue. In the depths of each is a spectrum mad enough to drive a person insane. He smells of lavender soothing my lucidity, pacifying my senses. We do not speak words yet we converse in depth. Our verbiage not unknown however, our profundity twists with confusion only we can decipher. He nods before taking flight as if reassurance were needed. He is the king of spring. Mountainous galactic glaciers with chartreuse hillsides pave his way.

Mascara drips down my cheek from my eyes, wet with springtime drippings. His sweat drips onto my skin, warm and welcoming. He glides inside me, showing glimpses of unknown places we have walked before. We are one in time and space; we are one disregarding physical contact.

.

A calamitous event it was, your birth. Suns moved within galaxies deep in the future yet far in the past. Enough that we need not be concerned with the darkness and death that lies just off cliff's edge. Enough that the subservience of this world constricts the supply needed for sustainability. We've skipped through lifetimes in the blink of an eye. We've allowed misconstrued earthly pressure and pleasure to alter our ultimate objective: progress.

Let me in the depths of the confines of your mind. I wish to hold you in place and protect you from the world. This place is dangerous and you are too powerful for it. Far removed from earthly games of words distorted embraces contorted. As the darkness brings forth light and the light settles to slumber within the dark, we are one. Mesmerizing mayhem leads to muddled melancholy at the mere meandering of the concave of my mind. Continue to feed me, Angel King and I will nourish you through and through until my earthly body serves me no longer and I move to the next place and the search for you begins again.

I hand you the watch, you receive it with your right hand. The time is stopped so we may savor the moment. Crescents fly past our viewpoint in convolutions, releasing clouded excretions of dead star matter. We perch atop the cliff, not a single word spoken, but a lifetime of conversations have been exchanged in silence. Do you recall our first encounter, Angel King? You have seen this in me before, and will see it time and time again in the wake of the world. We have taken turns guiding and following, never one more than the other. Spring-born equinox baby boy born in March; how would they know what you are?

Coiled caverns of my mind bring about perspectives entrenched in agony. Why have they perished, what have we done? Stars slated, your sword serrated our words into modern soliloquies with warm breath on my neck, my Angel King.

Why have you allowed this purgatory to be bestowed upon me? This crippling absence is debilitating. I'll meet you while you sleep my Demigod, I will brush your shoulder with my wing before taking night's flight once more.

I would rather live than merely just exist with you.

Sunrise, birds sing. Always with you, My Angel King...always with you, My Angel King!
Stand tall, cerulean blue eyes. Wipe the crust from healing wounds, refusing to disguise. Spiders weave the web of patience, she must adhere and remain, Gracious! Happiness debunked; blue sky defunct. Charcoal wings pearled slight, her mere existence a tumultuous plight. It was written before her time, this calamitous tale to spin violently into stratospheric resolve. Dark star matter, light, fractions, and prisms pain her eyes. No glass should bother to shield, for time merged with space, has been revealed. A sturdy mound she seeks to find, to rest her weary wings. For happiness is not her quest, existence is the song she sings.

Why did you have to die twice?

He explained how he enjoyed the rain. So, they went to where the rainforest meets the desert. She needed heat, he needed precipitation sifting onto his face like a feather dropped from his favorite avifauna. He could listen to them drop for hours, the rain.

He expected a little rain, unbeknownst to him she was a hurricane.

Unbeknownst to him, she was a wildfire.

Unbeknownst to him, she was a cyclone.

Unbeknownst to him, she was a storm.

Unbeknownst to him, she was a title wave.

Unbeknownst to him, she was a tsunami.

Unbeknownst to him, she was an earthquake.

Unbeknownst to him, I was a cocoon.

Known to him I am not a tornado. I am alone though; I'm surrounded by people.

Cocooned, shades of black and cerulean swirled together in synonyms union. Timeline switch, stopwatch click. Pained brown eyes full of angst, full of life. Affixed atop the highest tree branches bare imminent strife. Protect this life at any cost. The warm sun beats upon the branch with spears clenched tight to weaken grasp. It cracks. Spring has delivered on the equinox a winged male gift from a cocooned box. Eternal man with much to share, she sits aside him gentle glare. His immanence it pulls her in, she won't escape her shackled skin. The fibers of them are entwined, and the spoken words they are designed. They must sustain, they must remain, they won't outlive the hands of time.

Illicit in the eyes of those common foes. None related not fully satiated. Fill my mind with beautiful images and a thoughtful design. Take my hand, bring me beyond the edge. Expound upon the depths of our unknown to allow our progress to be shown. My earthly expectations are not existent, Angel King, for it is the before, during, and after here I am concerned with. Shower my consciousness with shards of stardust as if we play a private celestial game of target practice. Use your arrow to pierce me deeply, cause destruction with your bow. Your archery is synonymous with the release needed for progress.

Tactile textures, unknown to mortal men, separate us from the spinning vanes of the windmill's blade. Let the hourglass break as the sand trickles from one side to the next. Time could stand still while we search for answers in each other's eyes.

"One can only avoid the day by adhering to night." my Angel King said.

Let darkness reign over the light if it must. For the darkness is when I reunite with skeletal remains of those that tried and failed to captivate my Angel King. None before are relevant but one. Protecting the one with timeless moves of adoration requires separation to subdue the temptation that has caused annihilation and unforeseen obliteration. Each gilded dagger that pierced my skin was placed by those that fought for day, as it was I that fought for night, so that I may reunite to corroborate afflictions plight with Angel King. What's left? Two-star pieces, worthy of more than earth could yield. I held the gate. Spikes rained down like pelts of rain that surround my face. He does not waste another second and drapes his fractured wing over my skin to shield me from the wrath bestowed upon me for announcing that it is in fact I, the keeper of the gate. I recall the day like yesteryear, reminiscent of black holes, dying stars, and fields of ash that lie just beyond the edge.

Night billows the clouds in perfect not so perfect masses like graves of lost forgotten ones. The liquid droplets pierce my eyes with vibrant colors. The northern lights of azure, teal, and cerulean plastered against the jet-black sky. I feel at home but cannot decipher which course to embark upon. Degenerate dwarfs amidst the live circumvent a proper channel. I find the one that matches mine and hold tight to him as we circulate. I find that I need this one, and he pairs with me what is needed for progress. He exacerbates my every move and every thought. He makes me contemplate what is old and what is new, what is wrong and what is true. There is no other bound to me like that of my Angel King.

Let the fires that consume your imprisonment burn out of control. Let them melt the iron to ease you of your anguish. Let your dark heart bleed slow crimson droplets onto her. Leah, daughter of pain, goddess, Angel Queen. You're the sweetest night terror to ever wake me from fear's deepened sleep. But when I wake to find you're not aside me, day by day, my desolation grows exponentially. No metric to measure, no word to define. Melancholy midnight permanently rises with those that tire of trying. I'll never tire.

You amalgamate your light into my darkness. Skin shed as the caterpillar prepares for change. Wrapped tight in silky threads, enclosed slightly placed at the edge. The barren tree of which you hang, while weeks pass by, my timepiece rang. I click the watch to savor the day, for it may be the last I see of you before showcasing your gifts for all to see. The men grow angry, the women flock around. All desire a piece of this, my Angel King. I cannot restrict him; he is not mine to hoard. Jealousy has no place within our realm. Children get angry at attention splits, not gods and goddesses. I appreciate every second, every word, every utterance, every song from every bird that sings the songs of spring, my equinox-born boy.

With fractured thought, I set to fly. At cliff's edge, I seek the sky. Enthralled by night, I find comfort in the stars. My blue eyes peer deep inside and sever those that came before me, save for one. We stand aside both earth and Angel King, for earth and Angel Queen.

I'll be the night into your darkness.
I'll shine a light onto your dark heart.
I'll be the new bloom on your dying stem.
I'll have a role in your life's play.
I'm the sun-kissed skin after an outdoor day.

What if I told you I'm not worthy of you? What if your greatness surpasses mine? What if I'm merely a weak goddess still attached to earth? What if I have earth feelings I long to share?

I belong to none; you belong to one.

Stratus clouds reach for me like white widow legs. Patience is choked into my lobes like broken capillaries from a night session. It permeates and overtakes my senses. The indescribable feeling of missing one, embroiled in entanglement. Her nature was to end those that came before him, she spares him for he is unparalleled. Serenity's undisputed champion, he wears the belt. Hold my hand, travel back to the edge. Unlock the gate, I am the keeper. Spewed expressions like puzzle pieces yet to be placed in order. Angel King makes sense of the nonsense, collaborates, and creates mosaics of broken glass masterpieces day after day, after day after day...

Nestled high, she protects her home. From this vantage point, her optics are keen, she sees many things. She is aware of the possibilities and takes precautions to hold all close and safe. She knows she is in good hands; she is content with progress. It's the time of the night when the crescent's shining bright. The sky is full of colors but the stars are not in sight. They hide. Playing childish games of catch me if you can. I wait for them to saunter in so I may piece my course together.

When shooting stars, and dead suns of those that went before, she appears, she has no fears. She embraces all that was, is, and what will be. Patience is the lesson to learn. Restraint is a word she begins to use. White widow, take a mate, house him safe.

Unfold the new bright white straight jacket without fright. Rock in corners at earthly plight, throw boulders through the day into the night. Daggers in my eyes impair my sight. Prepare for battle, hold me tight.

Emptiness plagues me. Knowing I must go but none to go to. Knowing I must leave yet constant entrapment. I retreat and contemplate the wars won before us. How did we overcome obstacles of desire? How did we shift the hourglass on its side so time stands still even for a moment was a moment spent with you? What's it like to be in the presence of a God? What's it like to kneel before him as he encapsulates my consciousness and wrings it out to dry, then folds it into tiny origami birds and frees it in the sky? He's mine, he's ours, his existence divine. I've shared him for lifetimes, one more I'll entwine.

Fire rings unclosed; night demons exposed. True intent disclosed, Angel King composed. Release your labyrinth of turbulence unto me, I shall internalize it and regurgitate it back into strength for you. Gallop atop the mountain heading to cliff's edge. Stardust streaks before us, remembrance of home. The night sky is tranquil with you by my side, fear-removed eyes peer deeply inside. The universe is subservient to us from this vantage point. We feed from it, it replenishes our need for contentment.

At cliff's edge, I feel an icy breeze as I embrace a surge of heat. I look over the edge and see dead stars and black holes alongside stardust and strength. The electrodes that pulsate my fibers stimulate my sciatica and cause welcomed discomfort. Coveted in sleep paralysis I envelop myself in saris of silk embroidered in our skin tones. Whirlpools of emotion run their course bringing somber reflections of lives before. The night terrors plague sleep as deprivation ensues. I see you there, my friend, my lover, my partner. Who thought we'd be designed as pillars of safety for one another? Who knew that lock and key were essential to opening the box held so close and secure? We must entangle to decipher variations.

A storm made of wild and fire set ablaze atop the mountain. You and I step into the center of the flames. Only at this time do I feel complete. The ring can close and I'll be comfortable. The pillars of construct are unavoidable. The life outside the ring is not concerning. I see the trees, I hear the voices, they do not pertain to me. I have no apprehensiveness because I know I am safe and protected by you. The breeze is both blistering and bitter how is that so? For you and I bring both elements together convoluted, a perfect storm.

Look at the world: what a fucking calamity. People running around striving to keep up with others. I prefer to fly under the radar, away from the crowd, swim in the small pool with people like me. How is it that we see right through the murky waters and still persevere? Why do you suppose we have to separate? The pulse is too strong when we are one.

Imagine the fury that surrounds us in the eye of the beholders. Conceptualize what they see as they look tirelessly at their King and Queen.

Death proceeds life, as life succumbs to death. What is a tree without a seed? A seed must fall from a dying tree to be reborn upon the spring equinox rain and sleet-filled meadows of my waning heart. Oh, this tangled web, belonging to white widow muddled, with velvet crimson sticky threads intertwining past, present, and future. I am the past, I am the future, and sprinkled lightly onto the present.

Continuance is not only optimum but necessary. We must construct and simultaneously obliterate the pillars that imprison us. How fragile mortals are to attempt such incarceration. For in the blink of an eye, all could disappear.

Hands held, radiating frequencies. What a catastrophic coincidence that we were born at all. They know not of what we are set forth to accomplish.

For this is why they've tried to keep us apart, however, we always find each other.

Dim circumstances in a cruel and unknowing world. Universal turmoil, as footing, is consequential. The turbulence constructed as the timepiece ticks in absence of you my Angel King, in absence of you...My Angel King.

Crouched against the desert earth. Wings wrapped tight as I slowly recognize my existence. I'm exposed yet covered in the dust and debris of traitors and underlings. As I rise, my blue eyes shine as my stride is compromised. My feet lead with confidence in search of my Angel King. A far distance from here, he walks aside me simultaneously. He cracks tundra and glaciers. Not a night sky has passed in absence of him. It's been a lifetime we've been in pain, suffering our treacherous terrain in search to gaze upon which Angel is absent from us as we remain.

My mind is a menagerie of colors on a spectrum not exposed. Hues undisclosed, tints juxtaposed. Cerulean-draped Equinox-born Angel King, no shade to describe you in its entirety. The tastiest drink to sabotage my sobriety. One red pill to relieve my crippling anxiety.

You actually asked for him.
I heard the voice say, he is exactly as described.
Socratic questioning to calm my mind.
A different book I've yet to bind.
Sight from where I once was blind.

At cliff's edge, I peer over only to see waves crashing on the shore. The moonlight reflects off the water in blues and white set against the black dead sea. My Angel King reaches from his side, hand extended flecked, and pied. Within a snap of his finger, the sea flashed bright, he's brought the darkness from the light. As fog rolls in and dissipates, it's evident we've reached the gates.

Inside the imprisonment of my mind.

Eyes unfocused foreshadowed locusts and I can't see the forest through the rain.
The elements sift through me like a firestorm, but somehow, I still feel pain. Drowning sorrows, uncertain tomorrows and my mind wanders endlessly as I wane.
Searching for a reprieve with no tricks up my sleeve I watch quietly as he glides by. His shadow large as life, through death like struggled strife, my Angel King reaches back to dry my eye.

Light fragments shatter mirrored spectacles within my mind, I shiver at the sight. Tombs built with metal fabrics meant to bind, I worry for this plight. Midnight creek distorted current moonlight shined, I don't detest the blight. Jumbled speech, no recollection, vision blind. My grip is loosely tight. Fractured thought, inequitable remembrance. Memory hind, I welcome inflicted smite. Dangled pieces, future versions unrefined, the black is also white. Choking necks in painful pleasure devoured rind, I seek you so I write.

Sleepless nights siphoned memory merged with mine. Reach inside searching for the timeline twisted twine. Folded fabric beaded sequence yet to shine. Vineyards growing different fruits to turn into wine. Foliage forest green and dense with scent of pine.

At cliff's edge, you find me. Standing tall, confident in a black jeweled cloak and crying bodies. Approach slowly gasping as you view the carnage before we. Blonde mane draping down from the back, behind thee. You catch my eye as if to entertain their plea. The masses of those before us on bended knee.

Dark sky and billowing smoke fill the air. Cerulean capped stand firm looks that glare. Hand held out for comfort moments share. Midnight rainbow bright through night's despair. Cliff's edge, rough terrain optics rare. Angel King aside me as we stare.

Moments last lifetimes as memories flood my psyche of yesteryear. Self-inflicted pain, suggesting I walk my own plank. Such a travesty is life, death brings clarity smothers strife.

Opalescent swirls as eyes turn back time. Stopwatch clicks with changes, slow and prime. Marked for him through desolate sublime. Why we're always ripped from the other not to know. Puppets frolic maddeningly enjoy the show. All the world's a high and we're the low. Curved tops blend in contrast along the sky. Gray clouds condense to shower and bring life. Cosmic explosion shatters in my mind. Rapturous emotion jolted spine.

Sleep takes me over like hypnosis, lethargic from the rain. Clouds spin above and lightly drench my window pane. The sounds of people making love in padded rooms shared jacket on the floor. Lights flicker off and on as cameras reel to catch the scene.

Fingertip scratch, it was I who set your wing ablaze, like match. You turn and leap from cliff's edge, looking back and disappear, that's what I fear. I shield my cerulean eyes from the fire that earth has caused. I spring forward to follow Angel King. I see the inferno before me. I trail close, rising heat felt juxtaposed. His arctic shell left undisclosed, he turns and meets my gaze.

Continuance has a cost. I'll pay any ransom to keep you close. Cold breath at winter's frost, Angel King's drug I'll overdose. Ease my pain when I am lost, speak to me in beauty's prose. Guided path with compass tossed, written words do not transpose.

His frame, all that I've sought. He's strong in his dominance. Arms wrapped tight do not let go, it has been lifetimes— he's all I know. Tongue-lashed fire breath singes every hair. I feel his wrath. My Demigod, My Angel King, My Dragon Man, his voices sing.

Catastrophic events erupted upon your birth and continue to this day. Lunar optics sealed the skies as equinox baby boy was welcomed on Wednesday.

My ascension has been from birth. A hot summer's day in July, I emerged. The stars aligned then moved out of the way to welcome me. Unknowing yet knowing too much. My eyes looked around knowing I'd been here before. I searched for comfort in the one that brought me forth, I couldn't. I searched for comfort in the ones before me, I couldn't. I knew from that moment I was alone; I've always been alone. A square peg trying to fit into a round hole. Impossible. Always strong, always curt, always alone.

An endless world is death. How sweet it is to slumber within the darkness pierced with shards that make me shiver, like leaping but my wings are severed. Digging into unknown territory, knowing exactly where I belong. I wish to shatter the light and ignite the dark.

Frigid air blows my hair, as I walk with folded arms, sans jacket looking through the frost for my Angel King. The frozen landscape is foreign and familiar altogether. I've been here searching for him before. I kiss your cheeks, your eyes, your face in remembrance of lives before when I'd do the same. I feel your heart, its hallowed beats. I long to beat like you, my Angel King.

Silently, white widow spins her web. Patience is all she knows. She's waited lifetimes to meet his gaze. She's climbed to the highest heights to find him. Reached through galaxies and stopped to rest in eclipsed meteor showers. Entangled in self-combustion I feel his touch. His fingertip a frozen brand as it traces figures on my back. His eyes like hollow holes of ice, he sees deep into my soul.

A memory imbued with poignance transformed before my eyes as I sleep. The sadness felt is that of loneliness uncured by stealthiness. In my desperate despair, I refine the algorithms of my mind. Every step I take toward you. Every eye I meet is you. Every breath I take with you. You are the light that burns bright on the tip of the coiled wicked wax. Keep flickering Angel King, I see how bright you shine.

Thorn ridged branches, painful to the touch. They've nothing on your hand upon my skin. Sirens ring as fires burn the scape. Holes widen as we mourn the fallen ones. Dive deep into the waters dark and bleak. Show sorrow for the empty and the meek. Peer through fractured glass at figures broken. Lend a godly ear to words unspoken. Angel King like none I've ever seen, rise tall and show your passion to your Queen.

Your voice is a lullaby to my ear. Each utterance reverberates through my mind. Speak softly, warm breaths when you're near. Strong hold a stronghold that we bind. Sweet brown-eyed spring equinox-born Demigod I feel you here. Your vibration is the safety that I find.

Standing on cliff's edge, looking down upon the valleys of my soul. Penetrate me with your mind and tell me of the place you once came from. Fire, pierce my eyes, freeze me with the havoc of your life. Punish me with your light, remind me of our truth to not divide.

Night stalks the wind. It circles my body with endless funnel clouds. They stop with momentary pulsing that electrifies my senses. Only my Angel King could know what I feel. This feeling is unrivaled, only for him. Lightning strikes the sky. It intoxicates my being with predominant bolts of voltage. I'm inebriated by his paralysis. He galvanizes my efforts and makes me desire to be better.

Equivocal thoughts plain as day.
Nightfall riddled with serpents near.
Steadfast words are what you say.
Bloodstains, red, you hold the shear.
Stitch me up to our dismay.
Kiss my wounds remove my fear.
Blanket sheet covers as we lay.
Crowned equinox-born Angel seer.
Hands clasp tight as not to stray.
Speak parables only for me to hear.

Born strong, like a waterfall is in the spring. Aggravated bites on my skin from my lover's sting. Was it you under the forest line in the trees? Cold front comes in and you are all I see. Ice-dipped branches, frigid air, and Angel King. Try to stand while eyes take flight with a broken wing. Peach skin melts with brown while bodies sing. Bells chime through fractured metals. Chorus sing.

I look back on the damage caused by my spin within the sun. Forged by the light, wing stamped back composed for flight. Grab hold, claws pierce his scaled skin as we tear off into the vibrant star-filled night. Impalpable swipes we take at fear-based tripe, nonetheless, it's always been you and I.

Claw marks across him as he penetrates my soul. Slashed skin in remembrance of night's passion and turmoil. Withering from time spent captivated by brown eyes.

This guy from LA...
He's much more—to my surprise.

Everybody knows there's no such prose as a black rose. Not touched or tampered or misconstrued. This flower would be altered if not pursued. But one grows wild, it's special for you. Repair my broken wing, my Angel King. Strengthen me with your words and show the light as mine has gone dim. I will follow you anywhere.

Where do we slumber when it's all done and over?
Where do we reign when the rain is akin with thunder?
Where do we blossom when the flowers asunder?
My knowledge of you, Angel King is like that of a dense, vast forest where I am the fairy that lights the trees aflame.
We're hot. They're half-lit.
This is how I know I was born to merge with you.
Alone we are strong, together we divide continents.
Alone we are strong, together we massacre millions.
Alone we are strong, together we crumble dynasties.
I choose together.

Dismantled stems from rock glass and hardened gems. Black stones emblazoned long cloaks and char smoke. Hand reached for comfort in a tailspin. He crowned me with a circlet fit rightly for his queen. He shot me with a brand of brand-new morphine. His eyes, a hollow hole albeit a dark scene. What is life when I've been promised a dark death?

Perspective change,
new vantage,
new gift.
You walk aside, new timeline, new shift.
You raise my pressure, new heartbeat, new lift.
Say you're a chef,
new flour,
no sift.
Stay close, new current, new drift.

You're worth it. You rescued me.

Adorned with metal, shackled with chains.

I thank you, Angel King, for bringing me the sun on a cloudy day.

I'd drown in your eyes a thousand times over, just to spend one night in your arms. I'd cut myself deep and drip crimson blood straight onto you once more just to show you how I love you. This distance tears me apart from my core, I'm softer when you're near.

Swiftly move past me and stop, Angel King. Brighten my days with celestial overflow from deep within. Bring solace to my ever-chaotic world. You dim my light; I need that for all of my days. You blind my sight; I want you in all of the ways.

I'd lie awake countless hours searching the cosmos for you.

Burn me to ashes so I may rise as a truer version of myself.

Complexities turn to tragedies.

That long desolate road is certainly walked alone.

Indestructible binary forces. Black roses coveted courses. Thorn prick crimson pours from wounds gashed as angels mourn. Connected by distance, deliverance in an instant. Warm breath sweeps my skin, as eyes of fire pierce within. Blood-stained encrusted cape, cloak, and dagger savage drape. Cocooned in tattered fabrics telling stories of days gone by. Keep telling the story, Angel King, I'm forever listening.

White widow spinning webs of solidarity as she entertains moments of clarity.

Broken glass-like ice shards, they know not who we are. They throw knives not petals before us. Sliced skin wears thin and armored cloaks as blood soaks. She's both Angel and Devil's food cake, sweet but hot to the taste. Sharp as a knife, never dull. Keep piling my plate high, I'm never full.

The icy sky at night.
Auroras bright we take flight.
Pussy wet,
dick inside it— feels tight.
You rescue me from death's dance on high heights.
You're worth the pain, I see galaxies when I look into your eyes.

Crippled float, offshoots a sunken boat.
Two pills, back alive, my antidote.
Blank verse, write me what's not wrote.
Existential thought paragraphs I promote.
Song sung, Angel Queen, a high note.
Wings wide, castle dark— a deep moat.
I write for you, Angel King, memory rote.
Keep warm, hold close— I devote.

It is your heart I seek, Angel King.

Your mind and heart beat in sync with mine.

The seasons we create are but magnificent funnel clouds of particles intertwined. Suckle from me to nourish your higher being.

Rise up fire winged formidable Angel King.

Death's wings fly high and dry my Angel King. No reprieve for earth feels what sorrow brings.
Hypnotized, my eyes blind as hymns ring. Pierced ears, my mind full as angels sing.

What is to make of the ocean if the water is murky with poison? Waves crash and move sediment below.
Blue brine that jumps timelines.
What's mine is yours and yours is mine, my shocked spine.

Scales tip, an unbalanced gift, a time shift. Angels fly like butterflies in the night sky.
Melancholic mood drips on wet cheek.
Terrain rough, majestic bluff is cliff's edge.

Save a note for me when you sing that song. The one that drives you to the edge and back again. Remember always what I say, you're not alone. Green-eyed raven-haired topped with burgundy. Let my red wine drip down your purity. Hold you close, diminish our insecurity.

The days and nights roll into weeks before us, my Angel King. I seek you, nonetheless, each second a little more than the last. You heighten my heights and brighten my brights. You soil the sand with Angel tears from far before and beyond these years. I see a man so wise when I peer into his tiger-stone eyes. Embrace my pained yet content mind and blindfold with restraints that bind. Sun-kissed skin, warm to the touch, pinch it slow, release earth's clutch.

And as I rise as a fiery Phoenix, may all mankind kneel before me.
When my Angel King emerges from the depths of my fire,
dripping wet from his ice-cold shell, allow the mortals to gasp upon his entrance.
His bright eyes torture and char me to my core.
I melt.

I'll find you at cliff's edge.
We'll frolic among the rocks.
I'll hide from you and wait for you to find me.
You croon and flow through me, the sweetest the deepest gash my ears have ever heard.

Have you ever watched a person die?
Well, I have and I no longer wonder why.
Dry tears as they wet cheeks from crying eyes.
Not sadness but relief for the one that said goodbye.
Last breath.
Exhale as death's angels fly.

Adorned with skulls, shackled with chains. Those that fall still fall before us, agonizing pains. Blood stains from small cuts, you pierced my veins. It's all a gamble.

Go big for small gains. You're my medicine, inject me and ease my pains.

Tighten up my jacket, and wreathed straps.

I'm still sane.

What plagues me is eternity, alone. I've walked this road before; I've seen this sky and breathed this air. But none like this with you before, aside you, I shall not despair. You shroud me with your armored cloak, protect me from unveiled hope. With hands around my neck, you choke. You love me with unfettered scope.

Fires burn, pearled crystals flick my skin— I feel the sting.
Like brands of ancient tribes, marked scars they bring. Deliberate scowl of anxious pent-up tears.
Apologetic rhetoric unveiled for years.
Collided timelines cover us with pale fabrics, wrapping us in cocoons of love.
Content with circumvented lust.

Your eyes, they hypnotize. Your touch is never too much.

I want to fuck you 'til the sun rises.

Counseled by an Angel,
Trapped in the sleeves of Earth.
Tousled in anger,
Overjoyed at imminent rebirth.
Opened eyes hypnotize,
As you gaze, I realize:
You've always been,
You always were,
You'll always be,
My Angel King.

Wrists tied with slip knots. Hold tight, I'll slip not. Never gone far but far gone, it's us that brought the sunrise and sunset and stars and seas to meet at one spot. A montage of everything that's lovely and ugly comparing it to us, you see. There's so much darkness in my sight, I've bottled what I must. I'll always keep it airtight.

Through this darkness, I see your light. You say I plague you; I dim your bright. Through this chaotic puzzle of circumstance, you still piece me together. Like glue, it was always you. When I was blind, you helped me see. When I was deaf, you heard for me. When I was wrapped in white with arms crossed across my chest, you set me free.

Crackled pain.

Emotions flow like black rain through my cold and weary heartbeat.

In time with rhythmic insanity, cleared for flight scattered along this winding path of life. Consider me a receptacle for your pain.

Unload and release it for me to sustain levers bent scales weighed no loss to gain doors closed.

No vacancy.

Alone again.

Burn me to ashes and watch me rise as the true version of myself. Wings spread wide as I engulf my love and shield him from earth's divisiveness. Complexities turn to tragedies. Cliff's edge is where I'd rather be. Watching from afar the calamity. Withheld from perpendicular praise, we scatter within this dark maze, only to find each other amidst love's daze.

Burning wings my Angel King. Infernos cast from his eyes.
Cryptic songs my Angel sings. Earth is ablaze when he flies.
Rapid beats my Angel brings. They know not what power lies.
Blinding lights my Angel slings. Through the ashes, we both rise.

Hearts beat like timepieces in sync. Timelines shift and retreat, move forward in high heat. Lips touch soft skin, bodies thrash ripped sheet.

Pinpointed on map— no delete.

Hand-crafted eyes widen— don't blink.

Your star was meant to light up the sky.
Yours was designed to be present in the absence of eternity.
Your shine, so bright, it renders me blind.
So rare it angers me kind.

When you fly, Angel King, fly beside me.
When you spread your wings to turn, make sure I'm turning too.

His heart and mind she misses!
His touch she longs for and sweet kisses!
His gaze and scent, earth's blisses!
They mustn't fall subject to life's remisses!

It's said he's too good to be true. Please don't make this statement a fact.

Chrome eyes heavy in pain.
Closed door, eyes still peer from the other side.
Cloud burst from underneath like combusted energies that facilitate earthly bliss, decimated as a result of your gifts. Please tell me your well has not run dry.

Eyes sunk in from too much crying.
Worn thin, too much lying.
False grin.
Cavernous caves lead warm-hearted within, contorted tailspin.
Stance brave inside the end I begin; all is lost but I win.

You said you could never forget me, EVER...well here is something to remind you just in case you've tried to forget.

1979, I didn't know you but I knew you'd be fine. I knew you'd live life; I knew you'd do time. You said a few things, my bad, you were lying. I was too focused on angels flying while all the while the real deal was dying. Now, I sit back contemplating and sighing, climbing to cliff's edge as heights high-ing. What you're selling, King I'm not buying. New opportunities I'm now vying. Shards of glass, I'm still crying. Stomach in knots as I roll past Knott's. Ralph Lauren billboard sky high, 91 freeway as I drive by.

Round robin, slow the speed of my heart.
Wings-tattered saw the end at the start.
Carte blanche, you thought it was best we should part.
You understood my mind, and that's a different level.
You cataract my blind, in that I didn't revel.
You choked my words unkind, and now mindsets disheveled.

Like BPD, you got me laughing, crying, and laughing again. Each day, a new me discovered and learning why you left.
I was down as far as could be and you thought it was a good idea to make a hard left.
Excused a situation as a reason, knowing what's best.

White widow slithered
Black rose withered
Angel Queen shivered

...lights out

Acknowledgments

The man on the receiving end of this collection is dear to me, he can light the darkest sky with nothing more than a blink. He lit my way. I'm forever grateful we crossed paths, again.

A Little More About the Author

In her very first book, poet Jami Lynne takes readers on a walk through the dark caverns of her mind. Angel King is a free-flowing collection of thoughts and poetry delivered as one-half of the dialogue between the author and her muse. May you enjoy the complexities and deep introspective saunter along cliff's edge.

Made in the USA
Columbia, SC
22 April 2024

75f5bcd6-3b24-43b5-9a80-0b55b5bafde9R02